MySELF Bookshelf

Zippy the Runner

By JiYu Kim

Illustrated by JeongHyeon Seon

Language Arts Consultant: Joy Cowley

NORWOOD HOUSE 🏠 PRESS

Chicago, Illinois

DEAR CAREGIVER   MySELF ▌▐ Bookshelf is a series of books that support children's social emotional learning. SEL has been proven to promote not only the development of self-awareness, responsibility, and positive relationships, but also academic achievement.

Current research reveals that the part of the brain that manages emotion is directly connected to the part of the brain that is used in cognitive tasks, such as: problem solving, logic, reasoning, and critical thinking—all of which are at the heart of learning.

SEL is also directly linked to what are referred to as 21st Century Skills: collaboration, communication, creativity, and critical thinking. MySELF Bookshelf offers an early start that will help children build the competencies for success in school and life.

In these delightful books, young children practice early reading skills while learning how to manage their own feelings and how to be considerate of other perspectives. Each book focuses on aspects of SEL that help children develop social competence that will benefit them in their relationships with others as well as in their school success. The charming characters in the stories model positive traits such as: responsibility, goal setting, determination, patience, and celebrating differences. At the end of each story, you will find a letter that highlights the positive traits and an activity or discussion to help your child apply SEL to his or her own life.

Above all, the most important part of the reading experience is to have fun and enjoy it!

Sincerely,

Shannon Cannon

Shannon Cannon, Ph.D.
Literacy and SEL Consultant

Norwood House Press • P.O. Box 316598 • Chicago, Illinois 60631
For more information about Norwood House Press please visit our website at www.norwoodhousepress.com or call 866-565-2900.

Shannon Cannon—Literacy and SEL Consultant
Joy Cowley—English Language Arts Consultant
Mary Lindeen—Consulting Editor

Library of Congress Cataloging-in-Publication Data
    Kim, JiYu.
     Zippy the runner / by JiYu Kim ; illustrated by JeongHyeon Seon.
        pages cm. -- (MySelf Bookshelf)
     Summary: "Zippy the runner loves to run. Although Zippy has a skinny body, short legs, and has never won a race, he never gives up. With the encouragement from his friends, Zippy keeps running, hoping that next time he will do better"-- Provided by publisher.
      ISBN 978-1-59953-647-7 (library edition : alk. paper) -- ISBN 978-1-60357-669-7 (ebook) [1. Running--Fiction. 2. Persistence--Fiction. 3. Hopefulness--Fiction. 4. Friendship--Fiction. 5. Zebras--Fiction.] I. Seon, JeongHyeon, illustrator. II. Title.
     PZ7.K55968Zip 2014
     [E]--dc23
                                        2014009395

Manufactured in the United States of America in Stevens Point, Wisconsin.
252N—072014

4

Zippy was a zebra who liked to run.
His body was skinny
and his legs were short,
but that didn't matter.
He still loved to run races.

Zippy never missed a race.
If he had a cold, he would run.
If his leg was sore, he would run.
He ran in the wind
and he ran in the rain.
But the results were always the same.

PAPPA GALLO

Zippy always finished last.
His friends used to say,
"It's okay. You did your best."

But when Zippy kept losing,
his friends said to him,
"Maybe running is not for you.
Why don't you take up painting?"

However, Zippy did not stop running.
When he finished last for the hundredth time,
his friends said, "Why do you still run?
Why don't you give it up?"

"I love running," Zippy told them.
"Even when I'm last, I love it."

Zippy did stretches,
drank some healthy spinach juice,
and then did some running practice.

As he ran around the path,
he saw Winnie the pig
sitting under a tree.
"You look sad," said Zippy.

"I am sad," said Winnie.
"I have never won a race.
You always come in last
so why do you still practice?"

14

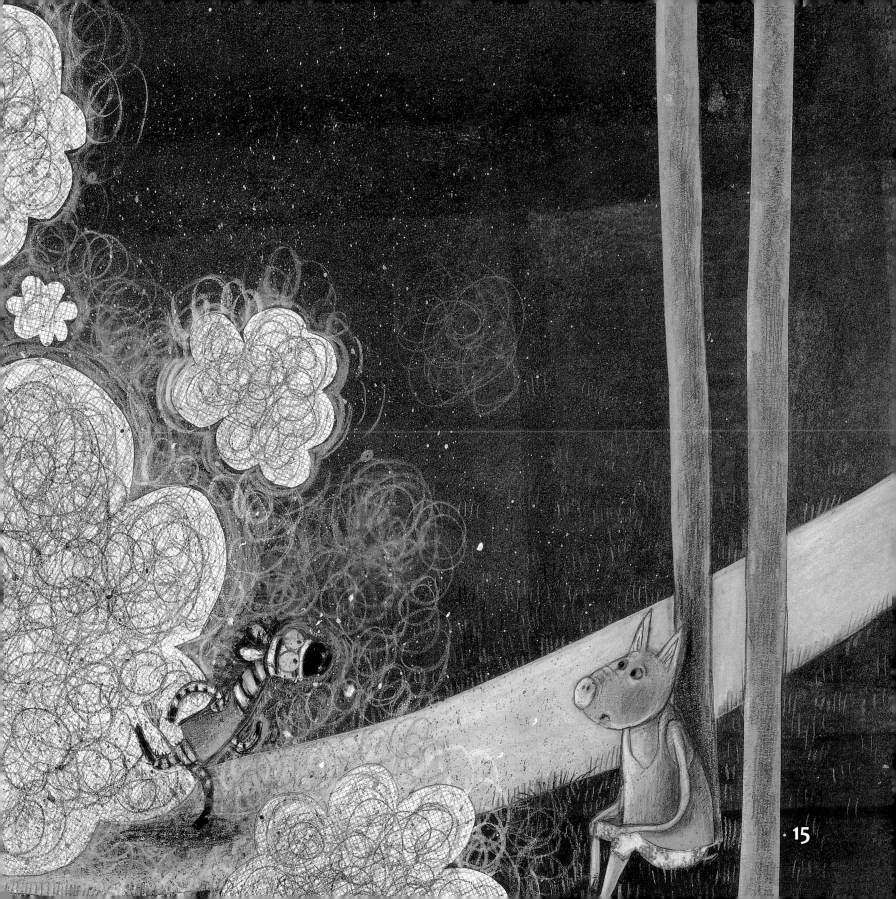

Zippy said, "I might be last now,
but I hope I can do better next time."

"What if you are last next time?"
asked Winnie the pig.

"There is always another next time,"
said Zippy. "The sun sets
and the sun rises again.
Hope is like the sun."

That night, under the moon,
Zippy and Winnie ran and ran
along the practice path.

18

The next time there was a race,
the friends said to each other,
"Good luck! Happy running!"

Bang!
The starting gun went off
and the animals ran like the wind,
kicking up clouds of dust.

Winnie crossed the finish line.
He was not first. He was not last.
He was in the middle.
And that was better
than he had ever done before.

But Zippy was in last place again.

When Zippy crossed the finish line,
his friends clapped and cheered.
"Zippy never gives up
even though he is last.
Zippy gives us all hope."

After that, Zippy's friends
began the **HOPE** running team.

Zippy runs with his friends
because he loves running
more than anything in the world.
He also wants to bring hope
to all those who finish last.

27

Dear Zippy,

Thank you for letting me practice my running with you.
I was ready to give up running.
You showed me how to keep trying.
I learned I should never give up
on something I love to do.
I will keep trying because
I might be able to do better next time.
You give me hope!

Your friend, Winnie the pig

SOCIAL AND EMOTIONAL LEARNING FOCUS

Perseverance and Having Hope

Zippy the zebra loved running. Even though he didn't win races, he kept practicing and always did his best. He knew that if he kept running, he would get even better. He had hope "like the sun." What do you hope for? What are your dreams? What do you love to do? A vision board can help you achieve your goals. Here is how you can create a vision board to remind you of all your hopes and dreams:

- Make a list of your goals, dreams, and wishes.

- Ask an adult for magazines that you can cut pictures and words from.

- Find pictures and words in the magazine that represent your hopes.

- Lay the pictures and words out on a poster.

- After you have arranged the pictures and words the way you like, you can glue them to the poster.

- If you can't find pictures or words in the magazines, you can draw and write them yourself. You can also ask an adult for photographs. If you have a computer, you can find pictures online and print them.

- You can add other decorations like ribbons and glitter, or drawings to make your vision board special to you.

Some people like to add quotes that inspire them. Here is an example from Walt Disney: "If you can dream it, you can do it."

Reader's Theater

Reader's Theater is an interactive approach to reading that allows students to understand each story through dramatic interpretation. By involving students in reading, listening, and speaking activities, they provide an integrated approach for students to develop fluency and comprehension. A Reader's Theater edition of this book is available online. You can access the script by scanning the QR code to the right or visit our website at:
http://www.norwoodhousepress.com/zippytherunner.aspx